# GROUNDED

# CHAPTER ONE

## THE SECRET'S OUT

**A** bright yellow family car cruised quietly along the near-deserted streets of Bellwood. Its headlights were on, shining like beacons in the evening gloom. Inside the car, perched behind the steering wheel, Sandra Tennyson glanced across at her husband, Karl.

'He's such a good boy,' she said, proudly.

Over in the passenger seat, Karl shook his head. 'Ben Tennyson is not a good boy,' he said. 'He's a great boy. I don't know if it's bad karma to pat ourselves on the back, Sandra, but we've done a pretty good job as parents.'

'Well, we haven't stifled him,' Sandra replied. 'Allowing a child to explore the wholeness of his entire being –'

## KRAAKA-BOOM!

With a blinding flash the road ahead of the car erupted. The explosion spat searing hot flames and thick, black smoke into the air, and shattered the windows of the houses all around.

Screaming, Sandra yanked hard on the steering wheel and stamped down on the brake. The car banked up on to two wheels, before coming to a stop just a few metres from the flames.

Unclipping their seat belts, Sandra and Karl clambered from the car, holding up their arms to shield their faces from the heat. As they watched the fire burn, they noticed something moving within it. An enormous figure stepped through the flames and fixed the Tennysons with a beady glare. Although Ben's parents couldn't possibly have known, they'd just seen their very first HighBreed!

The towering alien advanced menacingly, his gaze still locked on the Tennysons. Before he could attack though, a blast of pink energy smashed against the side of his skull. The power blast didn't hurt the HighBreed, but it certainly got his attention, giving Sandra and Karl the chance to escape.

Hand in hand they ran, abandoning the car as they tried to put as much distance between themselves and the alien as possible. As they ran, they spotted a boy on the other side of the street. He was running in the opposite direction, headed straight for danger!

'Hey, kid,' called Karl, 'you're going the wrong . . .'

Karl's voice trailed off when he got a better look at the boy. He recognised that brown hair, that green jacket, and that fancy watch. 'Ben?'

Forgetting the danger, Karl and Sandra turned on the spot and ran after their son.

'Ben!' cried Sandra.

'Stop!' shouted Karl. But the crackling of the fire and the booming of the HighBreed's heavy footsteps meant Ben didn't hear them. All Karl and Sandra could do was look on, as Ben slammed his hand down on his watch and an incredible transformation took place.

They had never seen anything like it. Ben's whole body was wrapped in a spooky green glow. His arms and legs began to grow, becoming longer, thicker and more powerful. His skin became green, and took on the texture of moss. A burst of red and yellow grew from the top of his head, giving the impression of flames.

'Swampfire!' he roared, racing up to face the HighBreed, who was now locked in battle with Gwen and Kevin.

Across the street, Ben's parents staggered to a stop. They looked at each other, neither one able to believe what they had just witnessed.

'Ben?' Sandra muttered, but the figure running into battle no longer looked anything like her son.

Unaware that his transformation had just been watched by his parents, Swampfire was closing in on the HighBreed. The big alien had his back to him, still focusing all his attention on

Gwen and Kevin.

'I grow weary of your pathetic human interference,' the HighBreed growled. With one hand he tore a lamp post free from the ground and raised it above his head. Before he could smash it down, a blast of searing hot fire melted the metal in his hands.

The HighBreed turned in time to see a figure streaking through the air towards him. Swampfire slammed into the big alien's chest, sending him toppling backwards on to the ground.

'You guys OK?' asked Swampfire, turning to Kevin and Gwen.

Further along the street, Karl and Sandra continued to watch, still barely able to believe their eyes. 'That's . . . Ben?' Karl muttered.

'Nice to see you,' Kevin said to Swampfire. 'You working flex hours now?'

It was Sandra who saw the HighBreed move. 'Ben, look out!' she screamed, but her warning came too late. The evil alien caught Swampfire with a double-fisted punch to the back of the head. The force of the blow lifted the hero off the ground. By the time he crunched down on to the concrete, Swampfire was barely conscious. A low groan escaped his lips, but otherwise he didn't move.

'No final words, Tennyson?' demanded the HighBreed, looming above his fallen foe. He flexed his powerful muscles. 'Still reeling from the augmented power of my new form, no doubt.'

'If you're saying you're uglier, you get no argument here,' said Kevin, stepping protectively in front of the fallen Swampfire. The HighBreed almost looked amused.

'I defeated Tennyson. What chance has the likes of you?'

'Me? Not much,' Kevin admitted. He pointed to a spot just a few metres behind the alien. 'But her . . .'

Gwen was in mid-air, running up a series of glowing energy stairs she had conjured up. As she drew level with the HighBreed's head she unleashed a wide beam of energy at the building beside him. A huge chunk of masonry broke off and came tumbling down on top of the alien, burying him beneath the crumbled stone and dust.

Touching down, Gwen let the energy fade from her fingertips. She and Kevin approached the mound of rubble. The dust cloud was beginning to settle, but otherwise nothing moved beneath the rocks.

Then, with a roar of rage, the HighBreed erupted up into the air, shrugging off the bricks and boulders as if they were feathers. He leapt upwards and hovered in the air several metres above the street.

'You've already wasted far too much of my valuable time,' he snarled, stabbing a finger towards them. 'I'll deal with you at my leisure.'

Gwen tensed, ready to launch another attack, but the HighBreed turned his back and sped off into the sky before she could even take aim.

'Kevin, Ben's still down,' she said, when she was sure the HighBreed wasn't going to double back and trick them. She and Kevin rushed over to where Swampfire was lying, just as he turned back into Ben.

One look at Ben's face was enough to make Kevin explode in a fit of laughter. 'Oh, man!' he snorted.

With a grunt of effort, Ben raised himself up on to his elbows. 'What?'

'The HighBreed gave you a black eye,' Kevin beamed. 'I like him better already.'

'Are you all right?' asked Gwen, helping her cousin to his feet.

'I'm fine. I just want to know where the HighBreed went. And what he's up to.'

'That way,' said Gwen, pointing in the direction the alien had flown.

Ben followed her finger. 'The waterfront.'

Gwen nodded. 'And he looked like a man

on a mission.'

'We'll meet at the wharf after dinner and homework,' Ben announced.

Kevin rolled his eyes. Homework. Ben was such a goody-two-shoes. 'Should I floss, too?' he sneered.

Gwen stepped closer and examined Ben's bruise. 'Your parents are going to freak out when they see that eye. How are you gonna explain it?'

'Not to worry, my folks believe anything I tell them,' said Ben, unaware that his parents had been watching the entire encounter with the HighBreed. 'I got this covered.'

# CHAPTER TWO

## NOTHING BUT THE TRUTH

**B**en stepped through the front door of his house and into the hallway. 'I'm home,' he cried, closing the door behind him. 'What's for dinner?'

He turned to find his parents waiting for him in the hall, their arms folded across their chests. They wore expressions he'd never really seen on them before, and he knew at once that something was wrong.

'What's up?' he said, putting on a smile.

'Where have you been, young man?' demanded Ben's mum.

'I was at the movies,' said Ben, thinking fast. 'With Julie. I know I should have told you. Sorry, I –'

'Karl, look at his eye!'

'That's quite a shiner,' nodded Ben's dad.

'If that was another few centimetres higher, you could have put your eye out.'

'Fine. I admit it. I got in a little fight,' said Ben, holding up his hands. 'It's no big deal. There was this guy at school and –'

'Ben, are you sure it was a kid at school?' quizzed his dad. 'And not a giant alien creature?'

That stopped Ben in his tracks. His mouth flapped open. Desperately he tried to think of a response, but none came to him.

'I can't believe it,' Ben's mum snapped.

'You look us straight in the eye and lie to us, over and over again.'

'We saw you, Ben,' Karl continued. 'We saw you turn into that thing.'

Ben tried to laugh. 'No, you just think you saw –'

Lunging, Karl caught hold of Ben's wrist and yanked his jacket sleeve up, revealing the glowing dial of the Omnitrix.

'I can explain,' Ben croaked.

His mum raised an eyebrow. 'Really?'

Swallowing hard, Ben looked from his mum to his dad and back again. 'Not so much,' he admitted. 'No.'

It had quickly become clear to Ben that there was no way of talking his way out of this one. He sat on the couch, his parents standing in front of him, glaring down as he told them everything.

'. . . which allows me to access the genetic code of various extraterrestrial forms in order to battle the DNAliens who will stop at nothing in their quest to take over the Earth.'

Ben's dad shook his head. 'And this became your job when, exactly?'

'Five years ago. Grandpa Max said we each have a responsibility to –'

'Oh, of course. Dad,' sighed Karl. 'I should've known. That's so typical.'

'He was more than just a plumber,' said Ben, rushing to Grandpa Max's defence. 'He –'

'Lied to us,' finished Ben's dad. 'Your Uncle Frank and I knew he had some other life. We knew. And that he lied to us about it all the time. I won't have you lying too.'

'It's our own fault,' said Sandra, fighting back tears. 'We were too permissive. And what did we get? A fifteen-year-old son needlessly risking his life.'

'Not needlessly, Mum,' argued Ben. 'It has to be me. The Omnitrix is attached to me. It doesn't come off.'

Karl narrowed his eyes and put his hands on his hips. 'Oh,' he began, 'it's coming off, all right.'

CLANK.

Ben's dad dropped a bent saw blade on to

the pile of buckled and broken tools that lay on the floor of his workshop.

'OK,' he admitted. 'It's not coming off.'

'I tried to tell you.'

Karl examined the Omnitrix on Ben's wrist. He had been trying to remove it for over an hour, using every tool in his toolbox. 'Not a scratch,' he muttered.

'Sorry about your saw blades.'

'In any case, you're forbidden from using the Omnitrix,' Ben's dad told him. 'Understand?'

'But Dad, all humanity is counting –'

A look from his father silenced Ben. 'Understand?' Karl growled, before leaving the workshop and slamming the door behind him.

Ben stood there, still reeling from the fact that his secret was out. Only the ringing of his mobile phone snapped him out of the daze. Flipping open the handset, he held it to his ear.

'This is not a good time, OK?

Down by the waterfront, Kevin and Gwen were lurking inside an old, run down shipyard office that stood halfway along a decrepit pier. Gwen was typing on the ancient computer, pulling up screen after screen of information.

Kevin stared at his mobile phone for a few seconds in disbelief, then snapped it shut. 'Uh, he said he'd call back,' Kevin muttered, walking over to join Gwen.

'Look at this,' she said, nodding towards the grubby screen. 'The logbooks show all these freighters as frequent visitors, bringing in goods, and shipping out local products.'

Kevin shrugged. 'So?'

Gwen pointed to some writing on the display. 'So this ship, the Eustacia Vye, is an unregistered tanker from the tiny island of Kastoon.'

'Where they used to do nuclear testing,'
said Kevin, adding, 'It was on the Historical
Channel,' when Gwen gave him a puzzled look.

'What would Bellwood be importing
from Kastoon?' Gwen pondered. 'And if it is
connected to the HighBreed, what would the
aliens want with it?'

Kevin gritted his teeth. 'Ask them,' he
said, turning towards the door, where a crowd
of DNAliens were surging in.

Brushing his fingertips against the
concrete floor, Kevin absorbed its strength. All

colour drained from his skin, replaced by the
dark grey of the stone. He hurled himself at
the first wave of the alien attackers, swinging
wildly with his fists as Gwen unleashed a
devastating series of power blasts.

Back in his bedroom, Ben moped on the
edge of the bed, his chin resting on his hands.
The sudden ringing of his phone made him sit
up.

'Yeah?' he sighed, snapping the handset
open.

Kevin's voice was edged with panic when
he spoke. 'Uh, hate to bother you, but we got a
problem.'

'You've got problems,' replied Ben. 'My
parents found out about the Omnitrix. I'm not
allowed to use it.'

'Folks mad at you, huh? Sounds rough,' said Kevin, trying not to sound too sarcastic. 'By the way, we're getting it handed to us by the DNAliens.'

Ben stood up. 'OK. I'm coming.'

Flipping the phone closed Ben hurried from the room. He took the stairs two at a time, his eyes locked on the front door. 'I've gotta go help Gwen with an after school project,' he shouted, still making for the exit.

'And it's homework?' called his mum in return.

'Yeah. I promised.'

'OK. Since you promised.'

Ben fought the urge to cheer. Instead he opened the door and fled out into the garden.

Ducking down the side of the house, he adjusted the dial of the Omnitrix, picked an alien, and slammed his hand down against the watch's face.

'Echo Echo!' he cried, as he transformed

into the small, wide-mouthed alien form.

Before he could run off to help his friends, a bright light was shone in Echo Echo's eyes. He squinted and saw that the light was coming from the beam of a torch – a torch held by Ben's dad, Karl. Behind her husband, Sandra crossed her arms and shook her head.

'Aw, man,' sighed Echo Echo, as he realised he had been well and truly caught in the act.

# CHAPTER THREE

## CAUGHT OUT

'Do you really think we're that gullible?'
Ben's mum demanded. 'We were
teenagers once too, you know?'

Ben's dad was lost for words. 'I really
don't know what to say.'

'Well I do!' Ben's mum snapped.
'Benjamin Tennyson, you are grounded.'

'What?' spluttered Echo Echo. 'You can't ground me. I'm a super-powered alien.'

'You're a super-powered alien who's about five minutes from forcing me to reconsider a lifelong disbelief in corporal punishment,' his mum replied.

'Up the stairs, young man,' added his dad.

Echo Echo considered arguing for a moment, but the expressions on his parents' faces told him he would be wasting his time. Grumbling below his breath, he trudged back inside the house and thudded up the stairs.

The little alien hopped up on to the bed and sat perched on the edge, kicking his feet and staring glumly at the floor. With a shrill beep, the mobile phone beside him began to ring.

'Hello?' he said, picking it up.

'Where are you?' cried Gwen from the other end of the phone. From the way she was breathing, it was clear that Gwen was running for her life. 'We have a little situation here.'

'And a lot of DNAliens,' bellowed a voice Echo Echo recognised as Kevin's.

Echo Echo thought for a moment. 'OK,' he said at last, 'aim the phone at them.'

Pausing for a few seconds to give Gwen a chance to take aim, Echo Echo drew in a deep breath, then unleashed a sonic shriek towards the mouthpiece of the phone.

Although he couldn't see it, Echo Echo's plan worked perfectly. As Gwen held up the phone the sonic blast screamed through the earpiece, scattering the DNAliens like skittles.

Echo Echo stopped shrieking and moved the phone back to his ear. Before he could speak, however, a hand snatched the mobile away.

'Who is this?' demanded his mum into the phone.

On the other side of the call, Gwen recognised the voice and instantly hung up. 'Lately,' she said, 'it seems like Ben's just been phoning it in.'

A few minutes later, Ben was back in human form, having just taken yet another telling off from his parents. He watched on, helplessly, as his mother slipped his mobile into her purse.

'That's my phone!' he protested.

'A mobile phone is a privilege, not a right,' his dad told him. 'You'll get it back when you've proven we can trust you.'

'Ben, are you hanging out with a bad crowd?' his mother quizzed.

'What? No.'

His dad joined in. 'Are they telling you it's cool to sneak out, turn into aliens, lie to your parents?'

'I want to know who this bad influence is,' his mum continued. 'Their parents need to know what's going on. Who?'

Ben crossed his arms, avoiding his mother's piercing glare. 'It's a sacred trust,' he said. 'I cannot divulge that information. Never, never, never!'

'You ratted me out?' cried Gwen, even before Ben had finished saying "Hello". He had been lying on his bed, idly fiddling with his computer, when the cordless home telephone had rung.

'I can explain,' he said, quickly.

'What's to explain?' Gwen snapped. 'My parents read me the Riot Act when I got home last night. "How dare you help Ben deceive your aunt and uncle, young lady?" Why did you tell them? You've gone nose to nose with Vilgax without blinking!'

'Vilgax never gave me the "mum look",' Ben replied. 'Sorry.'

'You're sorry, and I'm grounded,' said Gwen. 'Stuck here in the house instead of finding out what the HighBreed wants with that freighter.'

'Don't worry. Kevin's on it. He's going to check it tonight.'

'What?' gasped Gwen. 'You sent Kevin?'

Ben winced. By the sound of his cousin's voice, she wasn't happy that Kevin had been sent to investigate the HighBreed on his own. 'OK,' he said, hurriedly. 'I gotta go!' And with that – before Gwen could argue – he terminated the call.

The freight ship, the Eustacia Vye, sliced

through the waves, its decks laden with cargo. On board, concealed by a stack of crates, Kevin watched a lone DNAlien patrol the upper deck.

When the alien was safely past him, Kevin scrambled through a hatch, down a metal ladder, and into the bowels of the ship below.

'Uh,' he gasped, as a toxic stench burned at his nostrils. 'What stinks in here?'

He looked over the railings of the raised walkway he had landed on and spotted the source of the smell. Huge vats of green gloop bubbled below him, less than a metre from the walkway's edge.

Kevin reached into his pocket and pulled out a glass dish used for collecting scientific samples. 'Guess that's for Gwen to find out,' he mumbled, reaching out to try to scoop up some of the green ooze.

The sample dish stopped just a few centimetres from the surface of the goo. Kevin strained, trying to make his arm stretch just a little bit further. He raised himself on to his tiptoes, rocking unsteadily as he leaned over the metal railing.

### SPU-LODGE!

The green goo splashed noisily as Kevin lost his balance and fell head-first into the vat. 'Uh, it smells even worse up close,' he complained, kicking out with his feet as he tried to swim towards the edge of the tank.

From somewhere close by, he heard the clatter of running feet. The DNAliens had heard him fall in. They would be here any moment!

Meanwhile, Ben was sitting at the dining room table. He was eating dinner with his parents in silence – a silence broken by the sudden ringing of the telephone.

'Hello, Tennyson residence,' said Ben, rushing to answer the phone. 'This isn't a good time, Kevin,' he whispered, when he heard the voice on the other end of the line.

'You're telling me?' Kevin yelped. 'I'm up to my nose in smelly goo, trapped in a vat, and DNAliens are coming.'

Ben hit a button on the handset. 'I'm conferencing Gwen in,' he said.

There was a moment of silence, then Gwen's voice came on the line. 'Hello?'

'I can't get a grip on the wall,' Kevin told them. 'Uh-oh. Company.'

'Kevin?' asked Gwen, concerned. 'Is

that you?'

Right at that moment, Kevin couldn't answer. He was trying to climb his way free of the vat, but the slippery walls made it impossible. On the walkway above his head, dozens of DNAliens had just begun to appear.

'Absorb something and bust out of the tank,' Ben instructed over the phone.

'Absorb what? Stink?'

'What's your phone made of?'

'Titanium, why?' replied Kevin, before he realised what Ben was getting at. 'Oh!'

'Ben, you're on punishment,' said Ben's dad, setting down his knife and fork. 'Get off the phone.'

'One minute, Dad.'

'Guys, I think I know what Kevin's swimming in,' barked Gwen. Ben could hear the keys of her computer clicking as her fingers flew across them. 'According to Wifipedia, Kastoon has only one export. Bat guano.'

With a grunt, Kevin smashed his titanium fist through the side of the vat. The pressure of the goo forced the hole to open wider, allowing a slime-coated Kevin to slide out on to the floor.

'What is guano?' he asked, when his breath had returned.

'Evidently the berries on the island are radioactive from the nuke testing years ago,' Gwen continued, still reading from her screen. 'When they're eaten by the bats, the resulting waste is the rarest isotope in the world.'

Kevin grimaced. Resulting waste meant only one thing. He'd just been swimming in radioactive bat poo!

'Ben?' boomed his father.

'One minute!'

'The radiation is so mild, however, it would take a lot to constitute a threat,' continued Gwen.

A horrible thought struck Ben. 'Gwen, how much can that freighter carry?'

Ben heard Gwen's keys click a few more times. 'Fifty thousand tonnes,' she said at last.

Suddenly, Kevin's voice cut in, filled with urgency and panic. 'Guys?' he said, 'I could use a little help!'

ƆUUUUUUUUUH.

Ben pulled the receiver away from his ear and looked at it. The line had gone dead, but why? What had happened?

He looked down to see his mum's finger resting on the button. 'No phone means no phone,' she said, sternly. 'Go to your room.'

Ben rolled his eyes and headed for the stairs. 'I can't believe this is happening!'

# CHAPTER FOUR

# MAKING A STAND

**B**en entered his bedroom and threw his green jacket down on his bed. Only then did he notice an incoming call request blinking on his computer screen. With a click of the mouse, Kevin's metallic face appeared on screen.

'Hey, you found a wireless network,' said

Ben, smiling.

'Yeah. That's the good news,' Kevin nodded. He angled his phone so the camera pointed in the direction of an oncoming horde of DNAliens. 'The bad news? They're not happy about it.'

'Ladder,' barked Ben. 'Ahead on your right.'

Kevin looked around and spotted the ladder. He made a dash towards it, keeping the phone raised. 'Climb it,' Ben urged, scanning the screen as he tried to figure out an escape route. 'OK, the hatch on your left, go through it and hug the wall.'

Kevin did as he was told, ducking through the hatch and staying close to the wall as the DNAliens clattered along the corridor outside.

'Now just hang there for a second, 'til they pass' Ben whispered. 'Now back through and shut the hatch.'

'I get it, I get it,' said Kevin. 'You got a

real future as a personal navigation device,
Tennyson. Why d–' His voice dropped. 'Whoops.
Here come some more.'

'There's a crane hook right there,' said
Ben, pointing over Kevin's shoulder.

'What about it?

'Grab it. Then kick the green button.'

Kevin followed Ben's instructions to the
letter. The crane arm rose sharply, lifting him up
on to a higher deck. 'Whoa. OK, that was pretty
cool. I should roll solo more often.'

'Whatever. Just get out of there and
we'll . . .'

Kevin heard Ben's voice trail off. Even on
his tiny mobile phone screen, he couldn't miss
the horror in Ben's eyes. 'What's wrong?'

'Kevin, don't panic,' said Ben, as calmly
as he could manage. 'Everything will be OK.
Just –'

The towering shape of the HighBreed
stepped from the shadows behind Kevin. 'Nice

to see you again, vermin,' he snarled, catching
Kevin by the arm and yanking him into the air.

'Ben, a little help here!' Kevin cried,
before the image blinked out and Ben's
computer screen went black.

Spinning around in his chair, Ben saw his
dad finish pulling the computer's plug from the
wall.

'Dad, no!'

'Oh, don't you "no" me, Ben Tennyson.
You have defied us for the last time.'

'You've got to listen,' pleaded Ben,
jumping to his feet. He looked from his dad to
his mum, desperately trying to reason with
them. 'My friend is in trouble. I've got to go help
him.'

'I don't want to hear another word,' his
mum scowled. 'You are not leaving this room.
You are not calling anyone. You are not IMing
anyone. You are not texting anyone. You are not
My Facing anyone.'

'My Facing?'

'You will sit here alone until we tell you otherwise,' added Ben's dad. He let the computer plug fall to the floor. 'Understood?'

'You don't understand. This is a matter of life and death.'

'The only life we're concerned about is yours,' said Ben's dad. 'You're staying right here.'

'Don't look out there,' his mum said, when Ben glanced towards the window. 'Look at us.'

Ben glanced at the floor for a moment, collecting his thoughts. Slowly, he stood up. 'I'm sorry,' he said. 'I love you guys. You're awesome parents. You raised me by example. And time after time I've seen you put other people's needs first.'

Without looking down at it, Ben turned the control dial of the Omnitrix. 'I can't obey you now without disobeying everything you've ever taught me about life, the world and responsibility.'

'Ben,' glowered his mum, 'we forbid you to –'

'So when I get back, punish me however you want,' he said, cutting her short. 'But right now, I have a friend who's in trouble.'

With a slam of his hand, Ben activated the watch. His parents stepped back as he began to grow. And grow. And grow!

'Humungousaur!' he roared, as he

transformed into the hulking dinosaur alien. With one shove he knocked down half his bedroom wall, before leaping down into the garden below. 'Sorry,' he bellowed. 'I'll fix that later!' In the remains of Ben's bedroom, Sandra and Karl watched Humungousaur thunder off along the road. 'He just walked out on us,' Sandra gasped. 'What are we gonna do?'

Karl kept his eyes on the dino-alien until he was out of sight beyond a row of houses, then turned to his wife. 'We're going to listen to our son.'

Half a kilometre out to sea, a pair of powerful hands grabbed on to the outside railing of the Eustacia Vye cargo ship and began to pull. Almost immediately, the angular head of Humungousaur appeared above the railing, as the mighty alien hero heaved himself on board.

Screeching, a legion of DNAliens mounted an attack, hurling themselves at the intruder with all their strength.

Not that it did them any good.

With a single swing of his powerful tail, Humungousaur swept the aliens overboard, sending them splashing down into the crashing waves far below.

'You guys picked the wrong Humungousaur to gang up on,' he growled. 'I'm having a bad night.'

Down in the cargo hold, more DNAliens swarmed around. They buzzed across the floor, typing on computer terminals, checking cables, and studying tall glass tanks that were filled with the glowing green goo.

High above the floor, dangling from a series of wires, hung Kevin. He was back in human form, his whole body encased in a layer of the slimy ooze. On the walkway beside him, the HighBreed checked the controls of yet another complicated-looking computer terminal.

'This stinks,' Kevin muttered.

'You are not the first to taste defeat at our hands,' said the HighBreed. 'Nor will you be the last.'

'No, I mean the bat poop,' replied Kevin, grinning. 'I can't believe you eat that stuff.'

'We do not eat it, human,' snapped the

HighBreed, turning to face him.

'Sure you do,' insisted Kevin. 'What else would you do with it?'

The HighBreed opened his mouth to reply, then stopped himself. 'Tennyson has trained you well,' he said, 'but your pathetic attempt to learn our plan succeeded only in reminding me of the need to dispose of you.'

The alien's black talons swung out, snatching the cables holding Kevin and yanking the boy closer. Kevin gritted his teeth, but didn't look away. If he was going to die, then at least he would die with dignity.

**CRUNCH!**

The flailing form of a DNAlien thudded against the HighBreed's head, staggering him and forcing him to release his grip on the cables. Kevin broke into a broad smile as he swung back away from the walkway.

'I thought you got sent to your room without supper,' he said, as he watched

Humungousaur knock another group of
DNAliens on to their backs.

'Enjoy me while you can,' the dino-alien
grunted. 'I'm going to be grounded for the rest
of high school.'

Reaching over, Humungousaur took hold
of the cables holding Kevin and snapped them,
freeing his friend.

'I was just getting him to spill his guts
about his plans for the bat poop,' Kevin said,
wiping away the worst of the green gunk he
had been coated in.

'The DNAliens down there are rendering
it,' Humungousaur explained. 'Removing the
impurities until they're left with a highly volatile
isotope, suitable for use as a power source.'

Kevin raised an eyebrow. 'You figured all
that out by yourself.'

'Gwen,' Humungousaur admitted.
'Question is, power source for what?'

'It's a surprise,' hissed the HighBreed. He

was back on his feet now, and looking angry. 'The final surprise for the human race.' The giant alien stepped to the side, making room for dozens of his DNAlien minions to pass. They encircled the heroes, chittering excitedly in their strange alien tongue.

The HighBreed's face twisted into a wicked sneer. 'Destroy them!' he cried, and as one, the DNAliens attacked!

# CHAPTER FIVE

# A SURPRISE RESCUE

**K**evin gripped the metal railing, preparing to absorb its power.

'Hold up,' said Humungousaur, holding up part of the broken cable that had been holding Kevin. It was made of a strange alien metal, covered by wires and circuitry. 'Try this.'

Kevin's eyes lit up as he took hold of the cable and immediately began to change. 'Cool!'

There was no time to test out his new form, though. The first of the DNAliens had already begun hurling themselves into battle. They kicked, punched and spat, throwing everything they had against the two heroes.

One DNAlien was no problem for someone with the strength of Humungousaur. Ten, twelve, even fifteen wouldn't have given him too much to worry about. But there were fifty or more of the aliens attacking, and no matter how many the dinosaur alien knocked down, more rushed up to take their place.

Still the heroes battled on, Humungousaur lashing out with his tail, Kevin wading in with his fists. Before too long, the army of DNAliens had been vastly cut down in size.

The body of a fallen alien whistled past Humungousaur's head. He looked in the direction it had come from and met the gaze of the HighBreed. The evil alien had climbed down to the floor of the cargo hold, and was beckoning for Humungousaur to join him.

'Handle the rest,' the dino-alien told Kevin.

Kevin crunched a metal fist into a DNAlien's ribs and nodded. 'Do your thing.'

With a twitch of his powerful legs, Humungousaur leapt down to the floor below. The whole ship shook as he landed.

## KER-AKK!

The HighBreed swung out with a devastating punch, catching the alien hero off guard. Humungousaur hurtled backwards through the air, smashing through thick metal columns before slamming against the metal wall of one of the vats. The force of the impact drove him into the thick iron, bending it around him and pinning him in place.

Up on the walkway above, Kevin was still battling through the oncoming DNAliens. 'Might want to put some size on,' he advised, ducking to avoid a swinging kick.

'No room . . . in here,' wheezed Humungousaur, still fighting to get his breath back after the surprise attack.

'You look fatigued, vermin,' spat the HighBreed, stalking across the cargo hold floor to where the dino-alien was trapped. 'Let me help put you to rest, permanently.'

The HighBreed raised a fist, then brought

it down sharply on the side of Humungousaur's head. The force of the impact made the entire cargo hold tremble, and almost knocked Kevin off his feet.

As Kevin staggered, the DNAliens seized their chance. Throwing themselves at Kevin they caught him off guard, and quickly managed to wrestle him to the floor.

'Ben!' he cried, as he struggled helplessly against his attackers. But Ben had problems of his own to deal with.

The HighBreed fired another punch

against Humungousaur's head, snapping his powerful neck backwards. The evil alien cracked his knuckles. 'Congratulations,' he said, raising his fists to deliver a final, fatal blow. 'That was almost exercise.'

Humungousaur raised his head. A broad smile spread across his face. With a grunt of effort, he pulled himself free of the buckled metal and rolled to the side. A torrent of green goo gushed from within the damaged vat, hitting the HighBreed full in the face.

Still winded, Humungousaur launched himself towards the HighBreed, but the HighBreed was too fast. His powerful talons wrapped around the dino-alien's throat and lifted him clear of the ground.

Snarling with rage, the HighBreed hoisted the struggling Humungousaur above his head, then hurled him head-first to the floor. Swinging back his leg, he let fly with a thunderous kick that sent the alien hero rolling across the cargo hold. With a clang of metal, Humungousaur's head collided with a cast iron bulkhead door. The dinosaur-alien lay there, unmoving, as the HighBreed moved in for the kill.

One of those talons crept around Humungousaur's throat once again and began to squeeze. The HighBreed's other hand clenched into a tight fist.

'Goodbye, Ben Tennyson,' he cried, before the door at Humungousaur's back swished open and something shiny glinted in the darkness.

### BZZZZ-OOOM!

A blast of firey red energy struck the HighBreed on the chest and sent him catapulting backwards across the hold.

Just inside the open doorway, Ben's dad's finger relaxed on the trigger of the alien bazooka he held in his hands.

'Good shot, honey!' cried Ben's mum, patting her husband on the back.

'Like my dad always said,' smiled Karl.

'The right tool for the right job!'

Sandra dropped to her knees and cradled Humungousaur's head. 'Ben, are you OK?'

'Mum. Dad. Am I glad to see you!' the dino-alien yelped. 'I mean, I'm always glad to see you, but –'

'Uh, excuse me?' coughed Kevin, who was still buried beneath a mound of DNAliens.

'You're his ruffian friend, right?' said Sandra, accusingly.

'I've got it covered dear,' said her husband, taking aim with the bazooka.

'Whoa, whoa, whoa, whoa!' cried Kevin, suddenly terrified. The DNAliens were even more scared, though. Chittering in panic they jumped to their feet and fled along the walkway, leaving Kevin to drag himself back to his feet. 'Thanks,' he said, dusting himself down. 'Uh, nice piece, by the way.'

'Yeah, Dad,' frowned Humungousaur. 'Where'd you get that?'

'What, this old thing? It's been sitting in the attic ever since Frank and I were kids. Always hated it.'

Ben's mum rested a hand against her son's face. Humungousaur might not look much like Ben, but she knew he was still her boy inside. 'Fine, Mum. I'm sorry I just blew you off like that.'

'I'm not,' said Kevin, quickly. He was back in human form and walked up to join them. 'I mean, it's actually kind of cool that you showed up when you did.'

'It was very cool,' agreed Sandra. 'We're proud of you. Your friend was in danger. You had to help him.'

'His friend?' said Ben's Dad. 'You hear that monster, honey. The whole world was in danger. Ben saved it.'

'I helped!' Kevin protested, but no one was listening.

'The point is, son, we've seen you in action,' Karl continued. 'We know what you're capable of. Clearly, you know what you're doing.'

'You would've found a way to win even if your father hadn't shot the giant alien with the space bazooka,' added Ben's mum, helpfully.

As if on cue, the HighBreed raced from behind a stack of crates. Ben's dad took aim with the weapon, then went pale when he discovered the power source had been drained by that last shot.

'One sec,' smiled Humungousaur, taking

the bazooka from his dad's hands. Wielding the weapon like a baseball bat, he pulled back and swung at the HighBreed as he drew close.

Ben, Kevin and Ben's parents all watched as the HighBreed sailed up, up, up towards a bubbling tank of glowing green bat poo. The glass shattered as he smashed against it, showering the evil alien in a waterfall of the slimy gunk.

Ben's dad smiled up at his son and nodded his approval. 'Nice!'

An hour later, after they'd sunk the cargo ship and returned home, Ben watched his dad mount the alien bazooka on the wall above the fireplace.

'I thought you hated that thing?' he said.

'Yeah, I used to hate all of that plumber

stuff,' his dad nodded. 'It reminded me of the secret life your Grandpa Max hid from us. But now I understand he was only protecting us.'

In his mum's purse, Ben's mobile phone began to ring. Sandra took the phone out and glanced at the display. 'It's your cousin,' she said, passing the phone to Ben.

Ben took the phone, gratefully, then flipped it open. 'What's up?' he asked. Gwen's voice spoke urgently down the line. 'OK,' Ben said. 'Have to call you back.'

Closing over the phone he turned to his parents. 'So, there's been an alien sighting in the desert that –'

'Then what are you waiting for?' cried Karl.

Ben flashed his dad a broad smile, then raced for the door, only to find his mum blocking the way. Surely she wasn't going to ground him again?

'It's cold in the desert at night,' she said,

kissing him on the cheek. 'Take a jacket.'

Ben accepted the jacket, gave his mum a hug, then dashed out the door, ready to face whatever danger the universe might throw at him next.